For Alexander and Nicholas

Oxford University Press, Walton Street, Oxford OX2 6DP

Oxford New York Toronto
Delhi Bombay Calcutta Madras Karachi
Petaling Jaya Singapore Hong Kong Tokyo
Nairobi Dar es Salaam Cape Town
Melbourne Auckland

and associated companies in
Berlin Ibadan

Oxford is a trade mark of Oxford University Press

Reprinted 1988
First Printed in Paperback 1988
Reprinted 1989

British Library Cataloguing in Publication Data
Taylor, Anelise
Lights off, Lights on.
I. Title
823'.914[J]   PZ7
ISBN 0-19-279843-X (Hardback)
ISBN 0-19-272193-3 (Paperback)
Printed in Hong Kong

Anelise Taylor

Lights off

Lights on

Oxford University Press

Oxford Toronto Melbourne

When the lights are off
And the stars are out,
Only shadows move about.

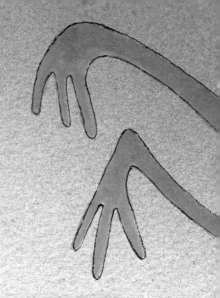

But do not fear
For they'll be gone,
When the switch is turned
And the lights are on.

When little Nicky went to bed

He pulled the sheet close to his head.
His cosy room, so warm and trim,
Held all the things that frightened him.

There's a stranger behind the door
I've seen him standing there before.
So tall and dark as he looks down. . .

Silly me! It's my dressing gown!

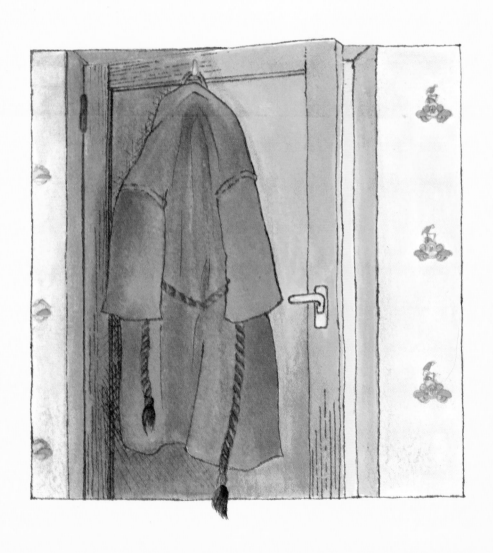

Is that a spider over there?
Hanging just above my chair.
Did I blink or did it crawl?

It's just a pattern on the wall.

Nicky closed his eyes to doze
'There's something moving near my toes.'
He felt himself begin to shake –
'Help! A creepy, crawly snake.'

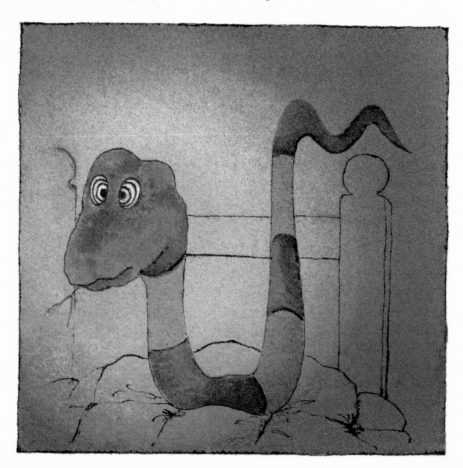

'Gosh, that gave me such a shock.'
'It's only my old football sock.'

There's something underneath my bed
With four large eyes and a furry head.
If only I could reach the light. . .

It's just my slippers – what a fright!

The wardrobe stands tall and wide,
There's someone hiding there inside.
Why am I afraid of that?

It's just my clothes, my coat and hat.

I see a shadow
But I'm not certain,
If something moved behind my curtain.
I'll just close my eyes and hide. . .

It's just the window, open wide.

Am I awake, or am I dreaming?
Is that a bird upon my ceiling?
There's no need to be afraid. . .

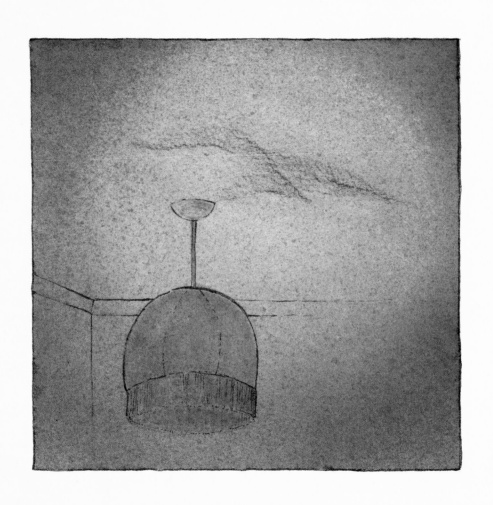

It's just the shadow of my shade.

I feel something touching me,
But it's so dark I cannot see.
Is there really someone there?

It's only Sam, my teddy bear.

On my cupboard
I can see,
Something looking down at me. . .

Just a minute,
That's not a face,
Only an old leather case.

When the lights are off
Things stay the same,
Only shadows play a game.

But do not fear
For they'll be gone,
When the switch is turned. . .

And the lights are on.

Good night.